Should We Squash Bugs?

by Ms. Caley's class
with Tony Stead

capstone
classroom

Some of us think it's good to squash bugs, but some of us think it's bad to squash bugs.

Onika and Aurelio think it's good to squash bugs because they could sting you.

leave me alone

Stone, Grant, and Emily think it's bad to squash bugs because they are living things.

Cyrus, Brooklyn, and Keana say, "Squash bugs because they are annoying!"

Crick Crick Crick
crick crick
crick

This is annoying

Ahhhhhhhhh!

Penelope, Isaac, and Max say, “Don’t squash bugs because they help us! Bees give us honey.”

Leigha, Seth, and Drake only squash bugs that can be harmful. They say flies should be squashed because they spread disease.

SKOosh It

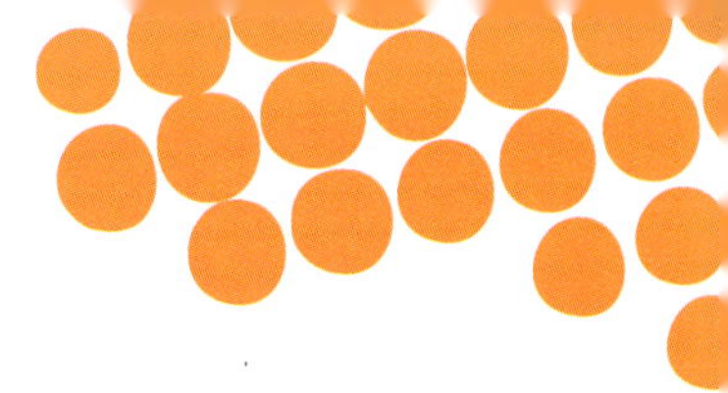

Hunter and Gavin squash spiders that come into their rooms because they are scared of them.

Haley and Naiya never squash bugs. They think they look interesting and that some of them are even beautiful.

So what do you think?
Should we squash bugs?